It was Ralphie's turn to take care
of Liz, the class pet, for the weekend.
"Don't worry, Liz," Ralphie said.
"You will be right at home with me!"

3

When he got home,
Ralphie remembered
something important.

4

"Liz, I left your habitat at school!" Ralphie cried. "Your habitat is your home. Every animal needs a home. What will you do without yours?"

Ralphie thought for a minute. Then he had an idea.

"You can stay in my room!" he said.

5

Liz did not like Ralphie's idea.
Ralphie thought some more.
"I will *make* you a new home," he said.
He looked out the window.
"Baby birds live in nests," Ralphie said.
"I'll make you a nest!"

Do you think a nest is a good home for Liz?

7

Liz did not like the nest.

8

"I guess a nest is not the best home for a lizard," Ralphie said. "Don't worry, Liz. I'll find you a home!"

Outside, Ralphie saw Dorothy Ann.
"How is Liz?" she asked.
"I left Liz's habitat at school," Ralphie
said. "Do you think she'd
like to stay in a rabbit
home instead?"

Dorothy Ann looked in the book she was carrying. "'Rabbits live in tunnels underground called warrens,'" she read.

Do you think a rabbit's warren is a good home for Liz?

11

Liz did not like the warren.

"I guess a warren is not the best home for a lizard," Ralphie said. "Don't worry, Liz. I'll find you a home!"

Ralphie and Dorothy Ann looked at a tree.
"Many squirrels live in holes in trees," Dorothy Ann said.
"Maybe that's just what Liz needs!" said Ralphie.

Do you think a hole in a tree is
a good home for Liz?

Liz did not like the hole.

"Maybe a hole in a tree is not
the best home for Liz," Ralphie said.
"Don't worry, Liz. I'll keep trying."

Ralphie needed to think. He made a snack to share with Dorothy Ann.

"I will *never* find a home for Liz," he said.

"Look, Ralphie," Dorothy Ann said. "Those ants are taking your sandwich to their anthill."

"That's it!" Ralphie cried. "I will make an anthill for Liz."

Do you think an anthill is
a good home for Liz?

Liz did not like the anthill.

"I guess an anthill is not the best home for a lizard," Dorothy Ann said.

Ralphie sighed. "Baby birds live in nests. Rabbits live in warrens. Squirrels live in holes in trees. And ants live in anthills. I guess different animals need different kinds of homes. But I still haven't figured out what kind of home Liz needs!"

"Dorothy Ann, does your book say anything about lizards?" Ralphie asked.

Dorothy Ann looked through her book.

"'Lizards live in many parts of the world,'" Dorothy Ann read. "'They like to live on trees, so they can eat juicy bugs. And they like to live near rocks, so they can warm themselves in the sun.'"

21

"Rocks? Did you say rocks?" Ralphie asked. "Look at Liz! She likes rocks!"

"That's true," Dorothy Ann said. "Liz likes things that other lizards do. But she's not an ordinary lizard. She needs the habitat we made for her in school."

"I know that," Ralphie said, "but I forgot to bring it home with me."

"It looks like Liz didn't forget," Dorothy Ann said.

"Liz's habitat!" Ralphie cried. "It was in her backpack all along."
"Liz's home is really something special," said Dorothy Ann.
Ralphie smiled. "That's because Liz is a really special lizard!"